AT LEAST A FISH

Anushka Ravishankar is a children's writer based in Chennai. She has written over twenty books for children, including *Moin and the Monster, Elephants Never Forget, Song of the Bookworm* and *To Market! To Market!* Several of her books have been translated into languages like Dutch, German, Italian and Spanish, among others.

The Lexile measure of this book (700L) represents the complexity
of the text. This Lexile measure—along with other characteristics of
the text, such as developmental level and subject matter—helps in selecting
books that best match a reader's level and goals. For more information on
using Lexile measures to connect readers with text, visit www.Lexile.com.

Lexile® and the Lexile logo are trademarks of MetaMetrics, Inc., and are
registered in the United States and abroad.

ZAIN & ANA

At Least a Fish

Anushka Ravishankar

Illustrations by Shilo Shiv Suleman

SCHOLASTIC
New York Toronto London Auckland
Sydney New Delhi Hong Kong

A Fish is Not a Dog

'At least a fish,' said Ana.

Her mother sighed. Her father looked sad.

That was not because the idea of buying a fish for his daughter made him unhappy. Mr Bopanna's face was like that. If he was not smiling, he looked tragic. His cheeks sagged, his lips drooped and his eyes looked like they were about to fill with tears. Luckily for the people around him, Mr Bopanna rarely stopped smiling.

Ana, on the other hand, was really sad. She had been trying for days to get her parents to adopt a dog. She had seen in the Young Readers section of the newspaper that there was a homeless litter of pups.

'Give one of these adorable pups a home, and get yourself a faithful friend for life!' said the ad.

'Pups are a nuisance,' said her mother.

'They're adorable! See, it says here, "adorable pups"!' said Ana.

But her mother refused. Mr Bopanna was always travelling, and Mrs Bopanna had to look after the home and Ana and her very demanding job. Almost three days a week they ended up eating cup noodles, because she didn't get home in time to let in the cook.

'I'm sure dogs like cup noodles!' argued Ana.

'They're not healthy! Thank goodness Zain's mother gives you healthy things to eat in the afternoon, otherwise you'd be having a very unbalanced diet.'

When Ana came back from school, she went with Zain to his house. Zain's mother looked after her until Mrs Bopanna got home. Every month Ana's mother gave Zain's mother a pretty little envelope with flowers printed on it. Ana thought it was probably a thank-you card for Abbas Aunty. She always looked so pleased when she got it.

Ana had been waiting for her father to come back from his business trip so that she could ask him to help her talk to her mother about the pup. But all that happened was that Mr Bopanna's smile disappeared.

'No,' he said, and stopped smiling.

So Ana got three fish instead of a dog.

Now a fish is very different from a dog. For one thing, it has no legs. It has a tail, which it sort-of wags, but it's not quite the same. You can't tell its mood from the way it wags its tail. A fish can't bark, it won't lick you all over the face and you can't cuddle it. Ana did try, but she got very wet. Because the biggest difference between a fish and a dog is that a fish lives in water.

Ana learnt all about how to keep the fish bowl clean, and how many pellets of fish food to drop into the bowl and how many times a day.

'It's ridiculous,' she told Zain.

Zain looked pained. He wished Ana wouldn't always use such big words.

'It is?' he asked, trying to guess what 'ridiculous' might mean. Good? Bad? Scary?

'Of course it is! I'm sure the poor things are starving. No wonder they're always opening and

Fish

Dog

Fish	Dog
No legs	has soft paws
No Tongue, Doesn't lick	Long tongue, can lic
Wags tail a bit	Wags tail a lot
Silent	Barks loudly
Wet	Dry

shutting their mouths. They want more food.'

'They do?' asked Zain.

'Of course they do! Wouldn't you want more food, if someone dropped a little ball of food for you, just once a day? Not even a ball, a little *marble* of food! A little *drop* of food!'

'I'd starve,' declared Zain. He ate lots of food, many times a day, and in spite of that, he was often hungry.

'See? Exactly. But when I tell my mother we should give poor Socrates, Plato and Aristotle more food, she refuses.'

'Why should you give Soc-whoever and Pluto and whoever more food? I thought it was the fish that were starving.'

'That's what they're called, silly. The fish. The ugly one is called Socrates, the fat one is called Plato and the other one is called Aristotle.'

Zain peered at the fish bowl. The three goldfish looked exactly the same to him. He wished again that Ana would keep things simple. If they were his fish, he would have called them, Fishyone Fishytwo and Fishythree. Or maybe Goldyone, Goldytwo and Goldythree. Why make life difficult with names which were impossible to pronounce? But Ana was right about one thing. The three fish looked like they were gulping and might die of starvation.

'I think you should give them more food,' he said.

'So do I. But my mother hides it,' said Ana.

'Give them something else then. What do fish eat? Seaweed! Give them seaweed,' said Zain.

Then he said, 'Oh.'

It had just occurred to him that the sea was about seven hours away. 'I know what! Give them spinach. I bet it tastes just like seaweed. They won't know the difference. They look pretty dumb anyway.'

Ana scowled. She didn't like anyone, even Zain, calling her fish dumb. She sometimes yelled at them because they were stupid and didn't wag

Socrates   Plato   Aristo

their tails or bark or do anything interesting. But no one else was allowed to call them dumb.

'They are not dumb!' she shouted. She went red in the face, and Zain got alarmed. He hated it when Ana lost her temper.

So he quickly said, 'I mean dumb, because they can't speak. Not stupid-dumb. Of course not! They look very intelligent. I think they must be geniuses.'

Ana took a deep breath. She recognised a peace offering when she saw it. 'Maybe they do speak. Maybe they have a language of their own and only they can hear each other.'

Zain pushed his nose against the glass and stared at the fish. They were opening and shutting their mouths. They reminded him of their band master, Mr Thomas. He did exactly the same thing when he was conducting the school band.

'I think they're talking to each other.'

Ana came to look. 'What do you think they're saying?'

'Mbmbmbmgllmb,' said Zain.

Zain was very good at this. He could make the strangest noises. He could whine like a dog, purr

Mbmbmbmgllmb
Do you suppose that Darwin had used a blah blah blah glug glug glug
What do you think about the metaphysic of blah blah glug?

like a cat, squeak like a mouse or caw like a crow. He could do the whoosh of a coconut tree and the glug of a sink as it got unplugged. He was always making noises and getting into trouble. So pretending to be a fish was easy.

'That means, "Where's the spinach?"' he explained.

Ana went to the refrigerator and pulled out all the vegetables. There was no spinach.

'Do you think coriander will do? We have lots of coriander.'

'Yup,' said Zain. 'As if they'll know the difference.'

Ana looked at him with dagger-eyes.

'Not because they're not clever!' Zain said quickly. 'But they've never tasted spinach, you know.'

So Ana and Zain chopped some coriander into little fish-sized bites and dropped them into the bowl. They drifted downwards in slow motion. Only Socrates came and poked at a passing strand with his nose. Then he turned away and ignored it.

'They don't like it,' said Ana. 'Now what?'

'We can go to the swimming pool and get some

weeds,' suggested Zain.

The 'swimming pool' was a dirty pond full of slimy water and weeds. It was a smelly and lonely place and the children didn't like to go there.

The story was that many years ago, the pond was used by the children in the locality to swim in. It had clean water, because it was fed by an underground spring. But suddenly it started getting smelly and stagnant. At around the same time, a boy called Chotu, who cleaned cars in the neighbourhood, disappeared.

People put two and two together, and came up with five. They whispered that Chotu was the cause of the spring being blocked. No one went in to check; they were afraid of what they might find. A few months later, Chotu reappeared, looking quite dry and unharmed. He'd been sick, he said.

By that time, the pond had become so filthy that no one went near it any more. Soon the area around the pond was overgrown with bushes and the only time children went there was when they were playing hide and seek, and someone was feeling particularly brave or desperate.

So Ana and Zain looked at each other with something like horror. Zain wished he hadn't made the suggestion. It had popped out without thought. Now one of them would have to admit they were scared.

Otherwise they would have to go to the swimming pool.

The Dragon in the Pool

'I'm not afraid,' said Ana.

'Me too,' said Zain.

Something scurried through the bushes.

'Maybe a little,' said Zain.

'A wee bit,' said Ana, 'but not much.'

The area around the pond was completely overgrown. The road was just a few feet away, but for some reason, this little patch of bush around the pool was like a world of its own. They could see nothing beyond it and all they could hear was a sinister rush of the breeze through the bushes, the whirr and buzz of insects that they couldn't see and the frightening suggestion of rat-like creatures that lurked in the undergrowth.

'What if there are snakes?' Zain whispered.

'Snakes don't do anything if you leave them alone,' Ana said, but her voice wobbled.

'What if we step on one of them by mistake?'

After that they slowed down quite a bit. Before he put his foot down, Zain made hooting noises, so that any snake in the grass would have the sense to move aside. Ana peered anxiously at the ground, squinting at every twig as if it might start slithering like a snake.

The bushes tore their clothes and scratched their skin. But Zain and Ana barely noticed. As they neared the pond, a foul smell began to fill the air, and when they reached it, they gasped. The smell was so horrible that they nearly turned and ran. But though Ana was turning slightly green, Zain was made of sterner stuff. He held his nose with one hand, pinched Ana's nose with the other and used the grip to pull her forward with him.

'Mg mgg ggggg!' yelled Ana. She didn't want to open her mouth. 'Mmm gm mg mggg!'

She pushed Zain hard. He fell into the pool and disappeared.

For one moment, Ana thought the world had gone black, then slowly it turned to blue, then yellow, then it came back to its normal colours. She couldn't see Zain.

Ana wailed.

'Zain! Zain! Don't drown! Don't drown!'

Zain sat up. He had indescribable filth all over him.

'You can't drown in one and a half feet of water,' he said, and vomited. 'I drank some of it,' he gasped when he'd stopped. 'It must be poison. I might die.'

Ana started wailing again.

'Sorry! Sorry! Sorry!'

'Oh stop,' said Zain, as he came out, trailing weeds. He picked some of the weeds off his clothes. 'Here, we got the weeds, now let's go.'

They turned to go, when they heard a noise from the pool. They froze. It was a loud moan. They turned to look, expecting anything. There was nothing, but they saw a huge ripple, as if something had dived quickly into the pool.

'A fish,' said Ana.

'Glubble, glubble,' said Zain, imitating the noise they had heard after the moan. It was like some creature had come up for air and then dived back into the pool.

'A very big fish,' said Ana.

They stood for a moment, wondering if they should investigate.

'What if it's a monster? A dragon or something?' asked Zain.

'It could be anything,' said Ana. They looked at each other.

'RUN!' shouted Zain.

They ran. They forgot about the snakes that

might be hiding in the grass and the insects and rats that lurked in the bushes. They only thought of the huge gulping monster in the pool. They didn't stop until they fell, panting, on the muddy road. Ana was still holding on to the water weeds. Zain stank and was covered in slime.

'Sheeeeee!' said a nasal voice behind them.

'Yuuuuck!' said another nasal voice.

Ana gritted her teeth. Zain began to bray like a donkey.

'You sound like a donkey,' said the first nasal voice.

'You smell like a pig,' said the second nasal voice.

Ana turned around.

'And you two sound like you've escaped from a lunatic asylum and need brain transplants— preferably from apes, because those are the only ones that will match.'

The twins, Meena and Beena, looked more puzzled than offended. They hadn't understood much. Finally, some kind of understanding dawned.

'Is she calling us apes?' Meena asked Beena.

'I think she is. She also called us luna-something,' Beena said to Meena. 'I think that means mad.'

'That's rude,' said Meena to Ana.

'You were rude first! You said Zain smelled like a pig!'

'But he does!' said Beena.

Ana and Zain had to agree. The stench from Zain was quite unbearable. Meena and Beena sat down far away from Zain.

'You should have a bath,' said Meena, 'Quickly, otherwise the smell will enter your skin and never go away.'

'You'll be stinky forever,' giggled Beena.

Zain looked alarmed. Ana looked uncertain.

'I'll go home,' said Zain.

'But if your mum knows we went to the pool, we'll get into trouble!'

Meena and Beena gasped.

'The pool! Weren't you scared?'

'There's a dragon in the pool,' said Zain, not even stopping to think. 'It tried to attack us. I jumped into the pool and fought with it till it got so scared that it dived under the water and disappeared.'

Meena and Beena gasped again.

'You're so brave!' said Beena. Ana was not pleased.

'When Zain was trying to hit the dragon with a stick, I saw its tail coming out of the water. It was longer than the water pipe in school! It was thicker than … than this tree trunk! It was about to grab Zain with the tail, so I picked up a stone and threw it at the tail. That's how Zain escaped,' said Ana.

'But if I hadn't jumped into the pool, it would have eaten Ana up. It likes small girls, that's like ice-cream for dragons.'

Ana was about to wrestle Zain down to the ground and tell him to take back his words, but when she moved towards him, she nearly gagged.

'Eeeeuw! You stink!' she said instead. 'Go wash up.'

But Zain couldn't go home because then his mother would find out they'd been to the pool which was out of bounds. Meena and Beena came to the rescue. They took Zain and Ana to the wash area behind their house and Zain washed himself as well as he could with a piece of detergent bar.

Afterwards, the girls sat in the shade of a mango tree while Zain dried himself in the sun. He began to feel sleepy. He was drifting off into a dream about swimming in a pool. There was a dragon who lived in the pool, and it was crying in a moany kind of voice.

Zain sat up with a start. 'It's lonely!' he said. 'That's why it was moaning.'

Ana had been thinking about the moaning and the bubble too, so she knew at once what he was talking about.

'What?' chorused the twins.

But Zain and Ana didn't answer. They knew what they had to do.

A Letter to Adopt-a-pet

Mrs Bopanna sniffed. There was a strange smell in Ana's room. It seemed to be coming from the fish bowl, which was odd, because it was less than two days since she and Ana had cleaned it. She peered into the bowl. The water was murky and some dirty bits of weedy, grassy looking things were floating in it.

Aristotle looked pale and listless. He was hardly moving at all.

'Ana!' shrieked Mrs Bopanna. Ana woke up with a start. 'What are these things in the philosophers' bowl?'

Ana's mother had taken to calling the fish 'the philosophers'. She said they looked calm and thoughtful, as if they had a deep understanding of life. That's why she had suggested naming the fish after the three most famous Greek philosophers. Ana had agreed, and then shortened their names to Socky, Platty and Totty, but that was a secret between her and the fish.

'The-the bowl?' asked Ana. Her heart bumped. She had planned to wake up early and take out the leftover weeds before her mother noticed them. Now it was too late!

Her mother was pulling out the weeds and making horrible faces.

'These things stink! What are they?'

'I thought it might be nice for them to have some real plants inside. Just in case they felt like nibbling something, between meals and all that, you know.'

'We'll have to change the water, fast! Aristotle's looking a bit green about the gills.'

Ana went to take a look. 'Green' was an exaggeration, she felt, but Totty *was* looking a bit sickly. She pressed her nose to the glass, and he gave her a sad stare.

Mrs Bopanna had gone into panic mode and within minutes, the water was clean and free of smelly weeds. Totty didn't look much happier, but the other two, who had also looked a bit morose, suddenly seemed to brighten.

Ana kept a keen eye on Totty all day. She made encouraging noises and waved colourful things at him through the glass to cheer him up. By evening she felt he was looking better. She thought he even smiled when she bounced her bright yellow smiley ball off the side of the bowl.

Zain had gone to visit his grandmother, as he did every Sunday, so she hadn't seen him all day. She was bored. She had finished reading two books

and one comic. She had used up her television quota for the week because she had watched a movie a few days ago, so there was nothing else she could do.

'If I had a dog—' she began.

Her mother cut in quickly. 'Why don't you go play with the twins?'

It was better than sitting indoors, so Ana trudged over to the twins' house. Her mother watched from the balcony till Ana had reached and waved. That was her signal to show that someone had opened the door.

Meena and Beena were overjoyed to see her. They were in the backyard, under the mango tree, playing with their kitchen set. Ana groaned. She knew she'd be forced into some silly drama now. She'd have to be an uncle who came visiting, or someone's lazy husband or someone's interfering grandmother. She decided to take things into her own hands. If she had to play house-house, she'd rather play it her way.

Zain wandered over a little later, and interrupted a tale of blood and gore: Beena was a fisherman who went to sea in a big bucket. Meena was the fisherman's wife who stayed at home to make a huge meal for her husband. Ana was a monster who lived in the sea. The sea monster caught Beena's bucket-boat, ate it in one gulp and then tore Beena limb from limb.

When Zain reached, Meena was complaining loudly that the food was getting cold and Beena was rolling on the ground and giggling helplessly because Ana had butted her in the stomach, and

she was ticklish. Ana stood over Beena looking disgusted.

'You can't laugh when you're being eaten by a monster,' she said.

'I c–can't help it,' Beena gasped, 'you tickled me!'

'I've had enough of this silly game,' said Ana. 'Let's play something else.'

"I made so much food! Who'll eat it now?' asked Meena.

Zain offered to help her finish it, but when he realised that the 'food' was cutlets made of mud and chapatis cut out of newspaper, he made vomiting noises and refused.

'What should we do now?' asked Beena, sitting up with a loud sniff and a big leftover grin.

But Ana had found a bit of newspaper and was bent over it. She wiped out the mud and held it up.

'One left! See? Isn't it adorable?'

The others came close. If they looked really hard, they could see through the mud on the paper. It was the picture of something. They could read some of the words ' ... pup ... one ... ador ... orpha ...' They guessed that the picture was that of a pup, but Zain thought it looked more like a gorilla. 'Adorable' was not the word he would have used for it. He didn't say that aloud though. Ana could be scary.

'I'm going to write to them,' said Ana.

'But your parents said you couldn't keep a pup in your house,' said Zain.

'It won't be in my house,' replied Ana. Beena had already run off to get a pen and paper.

Zain was alarmed. 'I can't keep it in my house!' he said. He'd been persuaded by Ana to keep a frog in his room once and he hadn't forgotten the fuss that had caused.

The frog had left a trail of destruction. It had frightened his sister Sameera so much that she had spilt her cocoa all over her new white PT uniform; it had leapt on to his mother's foot and she had tripped and fallen and fractured her little finger; and it had spilt ink all over his maths homework. It was the only time he had got a 'D' in his maths notebook and it pained him to think about it.

'We won't keep it in your house,' Ana said. But she wouldn't tell him what she meant to do. 'I'll think of something,' was all she would say.

Beena came with a pen and a piece of paper

torn from a notebook. She hadn't done a very good job of tearing it, but it would have to do.

Ana sat down to write the letter. Beena and Zain looked over her shoulder. Meena was busy feeding the mud cutlets to her dolls. The pink-faced dolls were quickly turning brown-faced.

Since she had nothing to keep the paper on, Ana propped up the piece of paper on the trunk of the mango tree. Which meant that she had to hold the ballpoint pen with the nib pointing up, so every now and then the pen would stop writing because the ink flowed away from the nib. The trunk was rough and uneven, so the paper kept tearing. Besides, after each line, Beena or Zain would have something to say which would lead to a long argument. Some of these arguments ended badly and people were hurt. The letter, therefore, took a very long time to write.

Dear Adopt-a-pet, wrote Ana.

'That's silly,' said Beena. 'You write a letter to a person. Adopt-a-pet is not a person.'

Ana chewed the tip of the pen. She hated to admit it but she could see that Beena had a point. But the advertisement didn't give the name of a person.

'I think you should just phone them,' said Zain. He'd been peering at the mud-smeared newspaper. 'There's a phone number.'

But Ana had already thought of that. She knew that they would never take a child seriously, and if she called, they would immediately know she was a child. But she could write like an adult, she knew she could. Her teachers were always telling her mother that she spoke like a grown-up, and that her language skills were excellent and her spelling ability was high.

But would a grown-up write a letter to a non-person? She didn't think so. Neither did Zain and Beena.

'Adopt-a-pet is a company,' said Zain, who knew all about such things. 'A company can't read a letter,' said Zain. 'Only people can read letters.'

Meena, when asked, said, 'What letter?' so she was left out of the letter-writing team.

Finally, after much argument and discussion, Ana wrote:

Dear whoever is in charge of reading letters at Adopt-a-pet,

This was because they had decided that in a

place as big and important as Adopt-a-pet must be, there would be a different person for each job. So there would be one person who wrote advertisements, one person who looked after the pets, one person who read the letters, one person who answered the letters and so on.

Ana went on:

I read in your newspaper that you have an adorable puppy which needs a home.

'Say "orphan puppy",' Zain suggested. So Ana put that in.

I have a home.

That seemed a bit short.

'With an extra room in which the puppy can stay,' said Beena.

'But that's lying!' said Ana.

'With plenty of place for puppies,' said Zain. 'That's true, at least. There is plenty of place. You could easily fit at least twenty puppies in your drawing room, if you kept them side by side. At least thirty.'

Ana thought about it. Zain was right. She wouldn't be lying. It wasn't her fault if they assumed that the puppies were going to stay in her home. She wasn't saying that the puppies would live there, only that there was enough place for them, which was true.

I have a home with plenty of place for a puppy.

The letter-writing went on for a long time. At the end of it, Ana, Zain and Beena were tired, sore and dirty from the thinking, the fist fights and the wrestling. Taking decisions was tiring work. But they looked proudly at the letter.

Dear Adopt-a-pet the person who is in charge of reading letters at Adopt-a-pet,

I read in your newspaper that you have an adorable orphan A puppy which needs a home.

I have a home with plenty of place for a puppy. It can run around and go to the toilet which is very clean and hygienic. So please send me the adorable orphan puppy and I will will take care of it if possible with proper pedigree food and a kennel A ible and everything. He will have my three fishes for company so he will never be lonely even when there is no ~~Please send the puppy to~~

~~Please send us your address so we can~~
~~come to your office and take the puppy~~
~~to my house which has plenty of place.~~

We already know your address because I have written this letter which we will send to your address which is on the newspaper. We cannot come to your office because it is very far away, but please send me the puppy at the earliest. I have already got a name for it, which is Superdog ~~Dogmatix Baingan Gorilla Veeru Hanuman Dingo~~ not properly confirmed ~~yet~~ but we will decide and confirm it before the orphan puppy comes.

Yours Obediently
~~A_____a~~ Bopanna

Fishing for a Dragon

Summer holidays were stressful for Zain's mother, Mrs Abbas. She had Ana at home all day, which was usually a good thing because it meant Zain was busy and wasn't moping around and complaining about being bored. But it also meant that the two friends were always up to something and she had to keep her ears and eyes open.

A few days ago they had tried to bring a cow into the house because they thought she was dying of sunstroke. It took a lot of vegetables and all her patience to get it out again.

And their dastardly plan to make a time bomb using an old watch and all the unused firecrackers they could find had been foiled just in time.

But the children seemed to be in a quiet mood

today. They had asked for an envelope—the stamped kind. She had asked them whom they were sending a letter to, but she hadn't been able to get a proper answer. Ana mumbled something about adorable orphans and Zain told her that it was a letter to a newspaper. Zain's mother thought it might be something Ana's mother had asked her to post, because Mrs Bopanna was the kind of person who wrote letters to newspapers, about bad roads or people cutting trees or temples and

mosques and churches putting on loudspeakers during festivals and disturbing everyone in the neighbourhood. Maybe she had written a letter to the paper about how orphans were being treated at the government orphanage.

So when the children asked if they could go and post the letter, she let them go.

'We'll be late, because we're going to Meena-Beena's house!' Zain shouted from the gate.

'It's not a lie,' he told Ana, after they had posted the letter, 'if we go there first. We won't tell them anything, we'll just go inside and come out again. We won't even see them.'

But he was wrong.

Meena and Beena were outside, playing hopscotch.

'Come and play with us!' they shouted when they saw Ana and Zain.

Ana and Zain turned around and ran. They ran into the bushes and kept running till they reached the pool. They didn't say anything but they both knew why they were running. They didn't want to give themselves a chance to be scared. Some things have to be done and it's best not to think too much about them.

When they were a few feet away from the pool, they stopped. The pool was still. No ripples, no glugs or gulps. The stink was still just as bad, but they decided to ignore it.

It was very quiet, except for the chirruping of insects and the occasional rustle in the undergrowth. They told themselves it was rats running in the bushes, because they didn't want to think of things sliding through the grass.

They could hear themselves pant, and it sounded as loud as Diwali crackers to them in the stillness of that place.

'What should we do?' asked Zain.

'Let me think,' said Ana, putting on her thinking face, which meant that she scowled and

chewed her lip and looked slightly mad.

Zain kept a respectful silence. Ana's thinking had led to some splendid ideas in the past. Most of them had ended badly, with both of them being punished and yelled at, but that was just bad luck.

'You could jump into the pool again,' said Ana at last.

Zain was not happy. He had had to hide his clothes in a plastic bag in the bottom shelf of his cupboard after the last time. He had sprayed half a bottle of perfume in his cupboard and all around his room so that the lingering stink would go. Now all his clothes smelt strongly of a powerful perfume called *Natasha*. Luckily it was a cheap perfume so his sister didn't make a fuss when she found the bottle almost empty. Unluckily, it was a terrible perfume (which was probably why it was cheap), so now Zain had to wander around all day with the strong smell of *Natasha* up his nose.

So Ana's suggestion made him whine.

'See, it's like this,' Ana said, ignoring his whining, though she secretly thought it was a perfect imitation of the dog that belonged to the school watchman. 'We don't know what makes it come up. So if we do exactly what we did the last time, it might come again.'

'I could push you instead,' said Zain. 'It's the same thing. We're almost the same size.'

There was a short fight. At the end of it, both Zain and Ana were tired and bruised, but they still couldn't decide who would be the bait for the

dragon. They lay on the ground, looking at the sun shining through the leaves. A crow sat above them and cawed, before it flew away.

Ana wiped the crow's droppings off her hand absent-mindedly. 'It's not that I'm scared,' she said, 'but I might fall sick. You know how easily I fall sick.'

Zain thought about this. The only time he remembered Ana being sort-of ill was when they'd got back from their school trip. And that was just a pain in her arm, because she had carried a big stone in her bag. It looked completely shapeless to Zain, but Ana said that it was an idol from an ancient temple and it was worth millions.

'You don't. I fall sick much more easily.' This

was true. Zain had all sorts of strange allergies and he never knew when something would make him sneeze and wheeze.

They argued quietly, too exhausted and hot to make another fight of it.

The first thing they heard was a sniffle. Then a nasal voice said, 'I'll tell Mummy.'

The same idea shot through both their minds. By the time Meena, her face streaked with dirt, tears and snot, came into view, with Beena dragging her along, Zain and Ana were crouched behind a bush near the edge of the pool.

'Meena or Beena?' whispered Zain.

'Whoever's nearest,' said Ana.

But the twins stayed at a safe distance from the pool.

'Let's go back, it's smelly. And we don't even know if they came here,' Meena whinged.

'They came this way. I know they're doing something. Otherwise why did they run away when they saw us? They must have found some treasure or something.' Then Beena gasped.

Meena screamed. 'What? What? What?'

'Shh! I just thought of something. Remember they said that they saw a dragon in the pool? When they came here maybe the dragon ate them up?'

Meena started howling and wanted to go back, but Beena stopped her. 'We have to see if we can find their ... their ... clothes or something. And don't make a noise. The dragon will hear.'

Meena refused to go towards the pool, even though Beena told her that the dragon must be full and wouldn't be hungry now. Somehow that only made her moan some more. But she didn't want to go back alone, so she waited behind a tree while Beena edged towards the pool. Beena was feeling less brave with every step she took to the pool.

When she was a couple of feet away from the pool, there was a loud yell from behind a bush, and many things happened at once.

Zain and Ana jumped on Beena and tried to push her into the pool. Beena grabbed Ana's hair in panic and fell backwards, taking Ana with her. Zain stumbled at the edge of the pool and landed in a heap, clutching at a plant to stop himself from sliding into the slime, and Meena, torn between fear for her life and fear for her twin, hurtled towards them, tripped over Zain and dived into the pool in a sort of flying leap. For a moment everybody was winded and nobody could make out quite what had happened.

Then there was a bloodcurdling scream from the pond and the three children sat up just in time to see Meena's face disappear into the water.

'Nothing will happen,' said Zain. 'The pool's very shallow.' But his voice wobbled.

They waited in silence for a second, then Beena, with a wail of terror jumped into the pond. Ana and Zain jumped in after her. The water was not deep at all; they were all standing in it, and yet, Meena seemed to have disappeared.

'We should go bring someone,' gulped Ana. 'Some … some grown-up.'

She had turned around to go when there was a whooshing and a slopping behind her, and suddenly, Meena's head appeared above the slimy water. She coughed and spluttered and vomited

and gasped, as they dragged her ashore. They were all crying now.

They fell in a heap several feet away from the pool and for a long time there was nothing to be heard but sobs and gulps and sniffs. Finally, when they had run out of tears and snot, they sat up and looked at Meena.

'There's a creature in the pool,' she said. 'It saved my life.'

Aristotle

Zain and Ana were in disgrace. Meena had whined and wailed and got the sympathy of all the adults because she had nearly drowned and Beena had managed to look like a saint because she had jumped in to rescue Meena, and also because Zain and Ana had jumped on her.

'Two good things have come out of this,' said Ana. She seemed perfectly satisfied with the morning's adventure.

'Two?' Zain couldn't see a single good thing in the whole business.

'Yes. Now we know that the dragon or monster or whatever it is exists and that it's a good dragon. And no one believed Meena when she told them about it. They all thought that she was so frightened that she had imagined things. So no one will go poking about in the pool and try to catch the dragon. Actually three.'

'Three what?'

'Three good things.'

'What's the third?' asked Zain, as he tried to stick a cloth up his nose to get rid of the smell of *Natasha*.

'The third is that your room has stopped stinking.'

Because, of course, the whole story had come out. The twins told their parents of Zain and Ana's first trip to the pool and Zain's packet of dirty clothes had gone into the wash with all the other slime-soaked clothes.

Zain began to protest that his room was not stinking, unless you counted *Natasha*, which he had to admit was quite hard to bear. But Ana had buried herself in a book. Zain sighed. Now he would have to find something to do on his own. Once Ana started reading, nothing would get through to her. He picked up a book and began to read. There was silence for a few hours.

Downstairs, Zain's mother told Ana's mother

about what the children had been up to during the day.

'I'm so sorry. They told me they were going to Meena-Beena's house. I didn't know ...'

'How could you? It's okay, really it is. I'll take Ana home and give her a proper talking to.'

But when they reached home all thought of scolding Ana flew out of Mrs Bopanna's mind. In the fish bowl, Aristotle was floating upside down.

Mrs Bopanna consoled a weeping Ana. When Ana's father came home later in the evening, he brought her a book by her favourite author. It was called *The Twits*. But even the sight of the book didn't stop Ana's tears. They tried talking to her and consoling her, but Ana sobbed and sobbed. They called Mrs Abbas and Zain was allowed to come and stay the night to keep Ana company.

'It's my fault,' she whispered to Zain. 'It's because of the smelly weeds.'

Zain thought about it. 'If it was just the weeds then they would have all gotten sick. But those two look quite healthy. Look!'

Ana looked. Socrates and Plato were swimming energetically. They were definitely in good health.

She sighed and felt the ball in her stomach get a little lighter. A few minutes later, when Mr Bopanna peeped into the room, both the children were fast asleep.

'I want to give him a proper burial,' Ana told her mother the next morning.

So Ana and Zain put Aristotle in a little cardboard box. They painted it and wrote 'Aristotle' on it in bright curly letters. In the corner, Ana wrote 'Totty' with a ballpoint pen, really small, so that only she knew that it was there.

Ana wanted to bury him near the pond, because she felt he would want to be near water. They were allowed to go on condition that they took Zain's sister Sameera with them. Sameera hated coming out of her room. She was always there, reading, listening to music or talking on the phone. But when she saw Ana's face she agreed and she threw herself into it with great enthusiasm.

Zain and Sameera's father had an old Mechano set. From the moment Sameera was old enough to hold a spoon, he had been trying to get his children to make things with it.

'When I was your age ...' he would begin. That

was the cue for the children to stop listening. He tried to get them interested by making complicated things with the set. But, of course, it was all too much pressure. The sight of the Mechano set always made Zain and Sameera feel slightly sick.

But today, Sameera took it out and she and Zain made a marvellous wheelbarrow with it.

They decorated it with little flags on which Zain had drawn the most beautiful fishes. They kept Aristotle's box on it and pulled it along with a string that they attached to it.

Ana went ahead and Zain and Sameera followed, singing songs, because Ana told them that she had read somewhere that that was what people did at funerals. They started with solemn and sad songs, but they ran out of those and so they began to sing all the songs that they knew. Since most of the songs they knew were happy ones, it quickly turned into quite a cheerful procession. Ana joined in and they were soon belting out the songs that they liked best. 'All izz well!' they yelled. 'Don't worry, be happy!' they warbled. 'Hey! Hey! Baby! Baby!' they sang.

When they passed the twins' house, Meena and Beena came to hang on the gate and watch them pass.

'We can't come with you,' said Meena. 'Our mummy told us you were bad children and we shouldn't play with you.'

'What are you doing?' asked Beena. Ana stuck out her tongue. 'I'll tell them that you're doing bad things again,' Beena shouted to their backs.

But Zain, Ana and Sameera were singing 'Bum bum boley' very loudly, and didn't hear her.

When they reached the pond and began to dig the hole for Aristotle, they were quiet again. They put the box in the hole, and stuck one of the flags that Zain had made, into the mud. Then Ana wept a little for the poor fish, and Sameera and Zain held her hands on either side and were sad.

It was while they stood quietly, looking down at the freshly-dug ground that they heard it. There was a long glugging sound and a swish of something diving into the water. They turned just in time to see something go down, but they couldn't make out what it was.

Holding hands, the three of them went towards the pool. Zain could feel his heart chugging somewhere near his neck. Ana could hardly breathe.

'What was that?' Sameera said in a normal voice. Ana and Zain jumped.

'Shhhh!' said Zain. 'It's the dragon.'

'It's an enormous dragon,' Ana added.

Sameera snorted. 'It's just a big fish,' she said.

But even she was slightly scared. Sameera had grown up hearing spooky stories about the pool. Of late people had lost interest in it, but when she was Zain's age, anything strange that happened always seemed to happen at the pool. The children used to run away when they saw poor Chotu, because there were stories about him and the pond which no one had ever heard, but everyone seemed to know. And yet, in all the tales she had heard, no one had ever mentioned a dragon.

Ana and Zain told her how they had first heard the dragon and how it had saved Meena's life.

'But Zain, you said the pool was shallow, so how could Meena have drowned in it? She must have been making it up. No one would have bothered to listen to her if she'd said she'd fallen in two feet of water. So I bet she made up all that about drowning and being saved. Sounds like hogwash to me.'

'Hogwash!' said Ana, liking the word. 'Hogwash. Hogwash.'

Zain glared at her. Then he looked at his sister.

'It must be deep in some places. It must be! Because even you saw the creature just now and it was huge, whatever it was. It can't live in a little bit of water,' he said. 'It'll need lots of water.'

They sat down and argued about how it could possibly happen that Beena, Zain and Ana walked on the bottom of the pool and Meena nearly drowned in it. Sameera was quite convinced that Meena was lying, but Zain and Ana had seen her disappear and appear again and they were sure the pool was deeper than it seemed.

'Look, this pool has been stagnant for years. There used to be a spring but it got blocked and people started dumping rubbish in it. So it's all filled up with rubbish. That's also why it's so shallow now. There's no way anything could live in there.'

But Sameera sounded uncertain. She had heard the loud 'glub!' and through the corner of her eye she had seen something. She couldn't imagine what it was. She didn't believe in silly childish stories about dragons or monsters.

'Nothing can live in there,' she said again. 'It's a dead pool, full of waste.'

Ana gasped. 'Must be a mutant monster!' she said.

Zain hopped up and down in admiration. 'Of course! Like the Teenage Mutant Ninja Turtles!'

'Yeah, right! So someone in the neighbourhood dumped their radioactive waste here which turned a fish into a dragon. You kids will believe anything you see on TV!'

'How do you know that only radioactive waste can do that?' asked Zain. 'What if … what if someone threw away their microwave?'

'Or batteries? Batteries have all sorts of chemicals!'

'Or cell phones!'

'Or computers!'

But Sameera had had enough. The pool was still now. If there had been anything in it, it didn't look like it would come back. 'Let's go home,' she said.

'We have to find out what it was,' Ana said. Zain nodded and made glugging noises.

'We'll come tomorrow. But you two had better not come alone. Anyway they won't let you.'

Zain and Ana realised she was right. They needed Sameera. So they spent the rest of the afternoon being nice to her. Sameera made them do all her chores while she lay around drinking roohafza and reading. By the end of the day, they were tired, irritated and restless.

How a fish can become a DRAGON

Fish

Radioactive Mutated Fish

Fish Dragon

Luckily for Ana, her mother thought her bad mood was because of Aristotle.

'I'm sure he's happy to be near the water,' she told Ana when she went to Zain's house to pick her up.

'Yes, but he must be lonely. Can we go and spend time with him tomorrow? Sameera said she'd come with us.'

'In that case …' said Mrs Bopanna looking at Mrs Abbas.

Mrs Abbas nodded. Behind their backs Zain and Ana did a gleeful thumbs up. They had planned to ask, but they had not expected it to be so easy.

Tragedy Queen

Dr Nirmala Joshi wished they had a better section on pets in the library. She looked at the books. There were about four or five books on dogs, a couple on cats, about half a dozen on different kinds of fishes, three on tortoises and turtles, several on birds—love birds, parrots, parakeets— and one, oddly enough, on platypuses. She had never heard of anyone having a platypus for a pet. It was probably dangerous.

She sighed and picked up one of the books. It was called *Fish and Foul: How to Keep your Fish Tank Clean and your Fish Healthy.* It had some very nice pictures in it. She sighed again. She didn't want a book on fish. What she wanted was a book on dogs. But she had already borrowed all of them and she

couldn't find what she needed. Because Buddhu was like no other dog. He was peculiar. What she needed was a book which was only about Buddhu, but she would have to write it herself.

She didn't think she was ever going to find a home for Buddhu. Two days ago, she'd got a letter and her hopes had soared. But when she read the letter, she didn't feel so hopeful.

'You almost found a home, Buddhu,' she told the puppy who sat before her with his tongue hanging out and a very silly look on his face. 'But they've forgotten to write their address, so how can I send them an adorable orphan pup? There's not even the slightest clue in the letter. All we know about the sender is that his or her name is A. Bopanna. That's an unusual name in these parts. We know that his or her home is large enough for a pup and we know that it is far away from here. Aha! We also know that A. Bopanna has three fishes. That's not much help. I can't see myself going from door to door asking people how many fishes they have. So Buddhuji, you'll have to wait till someone else wants an adorable orphan pup.'

Buddhu had wagged his tail and looked foolishly pleased.

'Do you keep fish?' asked a voice.

Dr Nirmala smiled at the woman who was standing next to her and looking at the book in her hands.

'I used to. But they all died.'

'Oh! I'm so relieved to hear that,' said the woman. 'Oh no, sorry, that sounded horrible, didn't it? How did they die? One of my daughter's fish just died and I've been feeling so guilty. I thought maybe I'd done something very wrong.'

'Unlikely. You can't go very wrong with fish. But you can't go very right either. You change the water, you give them exactly the right amount of food, and yet one day you find them floating upside down. It's very discouraging. Dogs are better. At least, most dogs.' She had suddenly remembered Buddhu. 'Here, you can take this book. I was looking for a book about difficult dogs.'

'Do you have a dog?'

'I have several, but there's this pup I found some time ago. He's a bit silly. Do you think dogs can have mental problems?'

'What kind of mental problems?'

'I'm not sure, but I think he thinks he's not a dog. I think he thinks … never mind, nobody would ever believe it. And it's only a guess. How can anyone know what goes on in that silly pup's head?'

'Pups are difficult to manage! I prefer fish. At least they're quiet and don't get in the way.'

'This pup is very sweet, though. I would keep him, but he upsets my other dogs. I've been trying to give him away,' said Dr Nirmala.

'You should advertise in the paper. My daughter's always finding that kind of thing in the Young Readers section of the paper. You'll probably get lots of interested people.'

'I tried that. A couple of people did come, but

Buddhu is … well … odd.'

The woman's phone began to ring. She picked it up and listened for a moment.

'Sorry, I have to go,' she said, moving away from Dr Nirmala, towards the check-out counter. 'You should say things like "adorable pup". That seems to work. Lovely meeting you!' she called out. A moment later she had gone.

Dr Nirmala stood still. Some bell was ringing in her head.

'Adorable pup. Adorable pup? I said that in my ad, but where have I heard that recently?'

Suddenly she remembered! The letter! Adorable orphan pup. And A. Bopanna had said that there were three fishes to keep the pup company! It was too much of a coincidence! Could it be that she had found the writer of the letter?

She rushed to the check-out counter and looked at the signature on the check-out sheet. It looked like a squiggle. There could be a 'B' there but then it might just as easily be

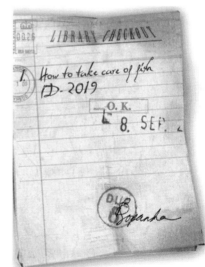

an 'S'. And was that 'n' or 'h'?

She asked the man at the counter for the name and address of the woman who had just left, but he refused.

'Madam, we have to protect our customers,' he said.

He looked gravely at her, as if he suspected that she might be the kind of person who took addresses of customers and then went to plant bombs in their houses.

Dr Nirmala looked him in the eye, trying to scare him into submission. She had grey hair, which made her look like a stern headmistress, and she was particularly good at looking people in the eye. That's what she did for a living.

But the clerk did not budge. He stood up straighter and looked righteous—like a man who would die doing his duty rather than give away the names of his customers to bossy ladies, however grey their hair might be.

He had underestimated this grey-haired lady. She was not defeated yet.

Dr Nirmala Joshi was an ophthalmologist by profession, but in her young days she had been the star of the P.K. Medical College Dramatics Club. She had been specially known for her ability to cry on stage. Meena Kumari, they used to call her. She could produce tears at the drop of a hat. She

TRAGEDY QUEEN

hadn't tried it in years. But it came back to her in an instant. It was like swimming or cycling—it didn't matter how long it had been since she'd done it.

The clerk at the counter looked aghast as tears began to stream down the cheeks of the lady who a minute ago had reminded him of his over-strict school principal. Dr Nirmala was proud of herself. The Tragedy Queen of P.K. Medical was still capable of a few tears.

People started to gather round. Several of them glared at the clerk who was looking at Dr Nirmala with his mouth open and a look of such misery that she wanted to pat him on the back and say, 'There, there.' She controlled herself.

One very scary-looking woman said, 'Aren't you ashamed of yourself? Making poor old ladies cry!'

Dr Nirmala wasn't too pleased at being called a 'poor old lady', but there wasn't much she could do about it. The woman put her arm around Dr Nirmala's shoulders. 'Don't worry, Aunty. I'll take care of him,' she said.

Dr Nirmala couldn't reply because she was choking. The scary woman smelt strongly of onion. There was no doubt that she would take care of the poor, terrified clerk. One blow of onion-breath on his face and he would probably fall unconscious.

Fortunately, it didn't come to that. The clerk quickly handed over a slip with the name and address of the lady who had just left.

Her name was Rohini Bopanna.

Operation Dragon

'We must have a plan,' said Zain. He was worried that Ana would get carried away and something horrible would happen. That they had to go and solve the mystery of the monster in the pool was certain. Neither Ana nor Zain had any doubts about that. Only Sameera felt it was a stupid thing to do.

'We'll call it Operation Dragon,' said Ana.

'Dragon-shmagon! It's a fish. A big fish, that's all,' Sameera said. But somewhere at the back of her mind was the memory of the thing that had dived into the pond, and it didn't look like a fish. 'There are no dragons, except in fairy tales,' she said weakly.

Zain and Ana gave her a sad look.

'Where do you think fairy tales came from?' Ana asked.

'From the imagination,' said Sameera.

'And where d'you think imagination comes from?' asked Zain, not wanting to be left out.

'Nice question, Zed for Zebra. From your head, that's where.'

When Sameera wanted to annoy Ana and Zain she called them A for Apple and Zed for Zebra. It didn't bother Ana very much, but Zain hated it. Today, though, he ignored it.

'But from where does it come into my head, then? From the real world, that's where.'

'Just because we can't find dragons any more doesn't mean they never existed. They must have become extinct,' said Ana.

'Like dodos,' said Zain, suddenly remembering Discovery Channel. 'Or dinosaurs.'

'Or pandas, when they all die. Then many years later someone will say, there's no such thing as a panda.'

'Some silly girl with holes in her cheeks,' said Zain, getting his revenge for the Zebra thing. Sameera had dimples so deep that you could stick pencils into them and they would stay there without falling off. Zain had tried it several times.

The argument went on and on, even when they'd collected all their things and were headed to the pond. They carried a mat to sit on, a basket with food and drink and some flowers for Aristotle's grave. In addition, Zain and Ana carried a torch (for no particular reason except that people in the books they read always seemed to carry torches), a rope (in case they had to tie up the dragon), a white flag which they had made out of Zain's new vest (so the dragon would know they came in peace) and some bandaids (in case of an emergency).

First, they threw the flowers into the pond. Sameera had brought a book to read, but she watched curiously as Zain and Ana did this.

'I thought the flowers were for Aristotle,' she said.

'Yes, but he's a fish, so his soul must have gone into the water. So I gave the flowers to his soul. Once the soul goes there's nothing left. That's what I read in one book,' said Ana.

'You read the strangest books,' said Sameera and got back to her story about a school for vampires.

She was vaguely aware that Zain and Ana were whispering, and every now and then the whispers got loud and there was a scuffle. But she was used to this. Finally, there was silence. She sighed and kept reading.

After a long time something began to bother her. There was altogether too much silence. She looked up. Zain and Ana were gone!

Sameera felt faint for a moment. A series of scenes flashed through her mind, like a fast-forwarded film: Ana and Zain walking through the water, both of them suddenly getting pulled down by their legs, Zain and Ana calling and calling to her while she read on without paying them any attention, Sameera wading in the water screaming out their names, Sameera running home to tell her mother, a search party with her parents and Ana's parents, everyone crying, the police arresting her for neglect, the court where the judge would ask her, 'Guilty or not guilty?', and she crying, 'Guilty! Guilty! Guilty!'

'SHHHHHH!' said a bush.

'Why're you making that strange noise?' asked another bush. The bush's voice sounded remarkably like Ana's.

Sameera collapsed on the mat making gulping, snorting sounds and even she didn't know whether she was laughing or crying. When she had recovered, she asked the bushes, 'What's going on? What're you doing?'

'We're disguised as bushes,' whispered Zain, very proud of his new word. 'Disguised. That means we're pretending to be bushes. And you got fooled! That means we've disguised very well.'

Sameera took a deep, calming breath. Her heartbeats were still quite loud. 'But why? Why're you disguised as bushes?'

'To fool the dragon, of course. So he'll come out thinking there's no one here.'

Sameera was quiet for a moment. Surely they weren't that dumb. 'But I'm here,' she said finally.

'Oh.'

'Oh.'

The bushes dropped their disguises and turned into two children who looked a lot like Ana and Zain. There was so much mud all over them and so many tears in their clothes and scratches on their skins that it was difficult to be sure.

All the disguising had made Zain and Ana very hungry. Zain started mewing like a starved kitten, and Ana's scowl became fiercer by the minute, because when she was hungry she got very irritable. Sameera was ravenous after the tension of the last few minutes. So the three children opened the tiffin boxes and began to gobble up the food that they had brought. There was pulao and puri and chana and jalebis.

After they had eaten and cleared everything up, Ana decided she was going to decorate Aristotle's grave. She had brought some bits of coloured paper, and she was going to stick them on sticks and put them on his grave. So while Sameera continued to read about the vampire school, Zain and Ana went to look for the grave.

They could not find it.

They thought they knew the spot, but when they dug there, all they found was a filthy broken saucer.

'It was closer to the water,' said Ana. 'It was here.' She dug and dug but there was nothing there.

They began to dig all around the spot where they thought Aristotle was, but they couldn't find his box anywhere.

Ana started howling. Zain tried to shush her.

'The dragon! The dragon!' he hissed, but Ana was past caring.

'TOTTYYY! Where are you?' she shouted, quite forgetting that Totty couldn't possibly get up and say, 'I'm here!' Not just because he was dead, but because fish don't talk.

Sameera dropped her vampires and came running to them. 'What is it? Why's she crying?' she asked Zain who was looking terrified. He was almost in tears himself.

'We can't find Aristotle!' he whispered hoarsely. 'Tell her to stop! The dragon will come!'

'Don't be silly, Zain,' said Sameera. 'You know there's no dragon-shmagon. Come, Ana, let's dig here. The mud looks fresh. This must be the place.'

'Nooooo,' wailed Ana. 'It was not here.'

Zain agreed. But Sameera had started digging, so they helped her, just for something to do. They were both sure this was not the place.

They were just about to give up when Sameera said, 'What's this?'

She was peering into a sort of hole within the hole they had made. Zain and Ana went to look over her shoulder.

There was complete silence.

Then Ana said in an awed voice: 'The dragon has laid eggs!'

Dog as Fish

Dr Nirmala looked sadly into Buddhu's eyes.

'It's not that I don't like you, Buddhu. I wish I could keep you.' Buddhu looked happily at her. He wagged his tail. But he did not bark. He hadn't barked once since she'd found him, the last and frailest of a litter of pups that belonged to a sick bitch that lived in the campus of the college where she taught a class once a week.

Some of the students had told her about the pups. Everyone knew that she had four dogs at home and that she regularly rescued pups and tried to find them homes. When she saw the litter, her heart sank. They looked like little rats. But with care and love and lots of milk, they had all become happy, frisky pups and had quickly found homes.

All but Buddhu. Buddhu was happy and frisky too, but he did not bark or whine. She assumed that he had been born with a physical problem but the vet told her that he was fine.

'Then why doesn't he bark?' she asked him.

'Who knows? I'm a physician, not a psychiatrist,' said the vet. 'You need to get his head examined.'

Dr Nirmala had walked off in a huff, but of late she had begun to think that the vet was right. Buddhu definitely needed his head examined. She hadn't dared to tell anyone this, but she had a terrible suspicion about Buddhu. There was no way to prove it. There was no way to find out what was going on in the silly dog's mind, but she was pretty sure she was right.

Buddhu thought he was a fish.

She'd seen the signs early, but she hadn't recognised them.

The other pups ate dog biscuits, bits of chicken and anything else that she gave them. Buddhu nibbled at the bread sometimes, but he didn't seem to enjoy anything very much, until one day he discovered the fish food that had been left over after the last of her fish had gone. He gobbled it up in one gulp before Dr Nirmala's horrified eyes and sat there with his tongue hanging out, looking so happy and satisfied that she began to buy fish food for him regularly. Maybe that was a mistake.

When she kept a bowl of water for the dogs, the other dogs and pups drank from it. Buddhu tried to jump into it. After he had nearly drowned in it four times, she had had to change the big common bowl for smaller separate bowls. Even then, Buddhu regularly jumped into them and toppled them. The other dogs were getting terribly upset with this.

He never barked, but he did wag his tail.

Lots of people came to Adopt-a-pet looking for a pup after seeing the advertisement. But when they tried to pick up Buddhu, and give him a cuddle, he was always wet. They didn't like that. And when they heard that he didn't bark, they left quickly.

Dr Nirmala was desperate. Her four other dogs were beginning to get very irritable. They pushed Buddhu away and she couldn't really blame them. If you're a dog, you don't really want a fish in your midst.

So Dr Nirmala was now taking active measures. She put Buddhu in the basket at the back of her scooter and zoomed off to find A. Bopanna of the letter. Some relative of Rohini Bopanna, she was quite sure. The Bopannas were used to taking care of fish, so they wouldn't find it difficult to take care of Buddhu, she decided.

Buddhu might have fishy delusions, but he was dog enough to enjoy the ride. He sat up in the basket and liked the way his ears blew backwards. He grinned happily and his tongue hung out in joy. He looked like a silly, happy puppy.

That was Ana's first sight of Buddhu.

Zain, Sameera and Ana were sitting on the roadside, just outside the bushes where the pool was. They were tired because they had run all the way.

When they had reached the road, huffing and puffing, Zain had asked, 'Why are we running?'

They had sat down right there and looked at each other, feeling very stupid. They didn't know. The sight of the dragon eggs had frightened them. They had quickly covered the hole and looked fearfully towards the pool. There was a ripple on the water. Ana, Zain and Sameera didn't stop to see what had caused the ripple. They ran.

'It was just the breeze,' said Sameera at last.

There was quite a breeze blowing. The bushes were shivering and sighing. The lone gulmohar tree was wiggling with the wind. Ana's hair couldn't make up its mind which way it wanted to blow. Some of it wanted to go one way and some of it another.

'What if the eggs hatch? There were hundreds of them. There'll be dragons everywhere,' said Zain.

'We have to do something,' said Ana.

'We'll have to tell someone,' said Sameera.

She should have known better. Zain, who a moment ago had been imagining dozens of dragons chasing him down the road, now stood up with Ana and looked angrily at his sister.

'Tell someone? Are you mad? They'll kill them!' Zain said.

'They must be the last dragons in the world! They're *precious*!' said Ana.

'We can find someone kind and sensible. Someone who likes dragons,' said Sameera, foolishly. She couldn't think of one adult who wouldn't panic at the thought of dragons.

'We'll just have to wait till they hatch,' said Ana, her voice only trembling very little at the idea of dozens and dozens of baby dragons crawling about the neighbourhood. 'If we touch them now, they might never hatch.'

'And once they hatch, what then?' asked Zain, feeling less pro-dragon by the minute.

They sat in silence, trying to think of a solution to the knotty problem. That was when they heard a loud VRROOOOM! They looked up, expecting a new-fangled motorbike, but what they saw was a bright orange, rickety-looking scooter hurtling noisily up the road. The woman riding it was almost off the seat, bent over like a racing cyclist. Behind her, in a big basket, sat the most silly-looking pup they had ever seen.

Ana looked at the basket and gasped. On the blue basket, written in bright yellow letters were the words, 'ADOPT-A-PET'.

When she saw the three children standing on the road and gaping at her, Dr Nirmala stopped.

'I'm looking for someone called A. Bopanna,' she said to them. 'Do you know her?'

'I'm A. Bopanna,' said Ana.

'Oh,' said Dr Nirmala. She had been expecting A. Bopanna to be a child, but this wild-haired, dirty-faced creature with torn clothes and scratched knees didn't look like she could take care of herself, let alone a troublesome dog like Buddhu.

'Is he the orphan dog?' asked Ana. 'He *is* adorable.'

Dr Nirmala got off the scooter, put it on the stand and sighed.

'He is. But you do know, A. Bopanna, that I can't give him to you till I've spoken to your mother. Is her name Rohini Bopanna?'

'How do you know?' asked Zain, astonished. He knew they hadn't mentioned it in the letter.

'Let's just say I have ways of knowing,' said Dr Nirmala, shamelessly pretending to be mysterious.

Ana frowned. She had made plans in her head of building a kennel for the adorable pup near the pond.

But now that they'd discovered the dragon eggs, that wouldn't be possible. And there was no way her mother would agree to keep the pup at home.

'They got me fish instead,' she said.

Dr Nirmala was not confused by the sudden jump from dogs to fishes. She knew exactly what Ana was talking about.

'Well, fish *are* easier to manage. They don't bark, they don't need to be cuddled or entertained, they don't need to be taken out for walks and they only need to be fed once a day.'

'What do you feed him?' asked Zain, who was trying to make friends with the pup in the basket.

'Erm … he eats fish food,' said Dr Nirmala.

Ana and Zain began to giggle.

'And is he toilet-trained?' asked Sameera. 'Does he bark when he has to go?'

'Erm … he doesn't bark.'

'Why? Is he dumb?' Ana asked. 'Doesn't he have vocal chords?'

Dr Nirmala looked at her in surprise and realised that Ana wasn't as wild and mad as she looked.

'See, that's the thing. He does have vocal

chords, but he still won't bark.'

'Take him to a vet,' suggested Zain.

'I did. The vet says it's all in his head.'

Ana and Zain looked at the pup's head. It looked perfectly normal. The pup was opening and closing his mouth soundlessly. It reminded Zain of something. He started imitating the pup, and making soft gulping sounds. Ana looked at him.

'You're right! That's exactly it.'

'What?' asked Zain. He still hadn't figured out what it all reminded him of.

'He thinks he's a fish,' said Ana.

Dr Nirmala sat down right there on the road and cried.

Zain, Sameera and Ana sat down with her. Sameera held her hand, Zain tapped her on the head repeatedly, and Ana sat across from her and said, 'Don't cry. Don't cry. Don't cry,' sounding more tearful by the minute.

Finally, Dr Nirmala gave a loud honk, wiped her streaming eyes and nose and grinned. The children took deep breaths and grinned back at her.

'I'm so happy to have met you, A. Bopanna.'

'My name is Ananya, but you can call me Ana.'

'And I'm Sameera and this is my brother Zain.'

'And my name is Dr Nirmala Joshi. I run Adopt-a-pet, and I've been trying for so long to find a house for this poor pup who thinks he's a fish.'

Then she told them all about Buddhu, his diving into water bowls, how he ate fish food and how she had once caught him trying to swim on the floor. The children were in splits by the time she had finished.

'I suspected that he thought he was a fish, but I

never dared tell anyone. They would have thought I was mad.'

'But I said it!'

'You did, Ana, and I wish I could give him to you, because you'll know how to take care of him. But I don't think your mother'll want a fish-dog in the house.' She sighed. 'Still, I'll meet her. Where is she?'

'She isn't back from work yet,' said Ana.

'Can we play with him till she comes?' asked Zain.

So Dr Nirmala took Buddhu out of the basket. But no sooner had she put him down than he shot off into the bushes like an arrow.

He had smelt the water.

'Oh no, now where's he gone off to?' said Dr Nirmala, not terribly worried. He was always wandering off and coming back.

But Zain, Ana and Sameera looked at each other in alarm.

'To the pool!' said Ana. 'And there's a dragon in it!'

Fish as Dog

When they reached the pool, the pup was wading happily into it.

'Buddhu! Come back!' called Dr Nirmala.

But the pup looked like he'd reached his idea of heaven. He splashed and swam out.

And then, suddenly, he disappeared. There was silence for a moment. Dr Nirmala hitched up her salwar and prepared to wade in. Sameera, Zain and Ana grabbed hold of her.

'You can't go!' said Zain. 'It's dangerous!'

'There's a dragon!'

'A dragon? What are you talking about?'

The children told her quickly about the dragon and its eggs. As they spoke, they kept looking anxiously for the pup, but it seemed to have gone.

Zain began to sob. 'What are we going to do?' he asked Dr Nirmala.

Sameera sniffled. 'We can't do anything.'

'Maybe he's really a fish and he's happy at last,' said Ana in a quivery voice and the others could tell that she almost believed it.

Dr Nirmala had tears running down her face. But when she spoke, her voice was firm. 'We have to do something,' she said. 'I'm going in.'

She started wading in. It seemed like hours, but it was actually just a little over a minute since the pup had disappeared. The three children fell quiet, as they watched Dr Nirmala walk into the pond. Then, in the silence, they heard a swishing, splashing sound. Dr Nirmala stopped. The children rushed to the edge of the pond.

And as they watched, they saw a strange sight. The pup, wet and bedraggled and unconscious, rose from the pool. It was lying on a beautifully patterned rock-like thing. As the thing rose higher, they saw it was the shell of an enormous turtle. The turtle waded through the pool towards them.

Dr Nirmala walked forward quickly and took

the pup off the turtle's gigantic back. The turtle stopped for a moment and looked at them with the wisest, oldest eyes any of them had ever seen. Then it turned and waded back through the pool. It dived in with a loud glug and a huge ripple, and it was gone.

Mesmerised, Ana, Zain and Sameera watched their dragon go.

Dr Nirmala, meanwhile, was trying to get the water out of the pup's lungs.

'Come on, Buddhu! Come back! Open your eyes, Buddhu!' she said, as she tried to suck out the water through the pup's mouth. At last, the pup choked and coughed and opened its eyes.

And then it barked a small hoarse bark.

'Buddhu! Buddhu! Buddhu!' cried Dr Nirmala, overjoyed.

'Why do you call him that?' asked Ana. 'That's not nice.'

'Because he's a silly dog, a real buddhu!' said Dr Nirmala fiercely, shaking the pup in a loving way. 'Silly, silly dog! Imagine jumping into the water as if you're some kind of fish.'

'It's alright to think you're something you're

not. Our teacher's always telling us to do it. It's called creative imagination.'

Dr Nirmala blinked and grinned. 'Creative imagination! You know, maybe you're right. Maybe he's not stupid, just different. So what do you think I should call him then?'

Zain and Ana had a whispered consultation. They told Sameera and Sameera laughed and nodded.

'Fish,' said Ana. 'You should call him Fish.'

Fish among Fish

'You're going to the pool again?' asked Meena.

'What about the dragon?' asked Beena.

Meena and Beena couldn't understand why Zain, Ana and Sameera were suddenly allowed to go to the pool so often. The pool had been out of bounds to the children for years.

Of late, something had started happening to the pool. The smell was getting less unbearable. The water was looking cleaner. But that was not why the children were going there. They were going to keep an eye on the dragon eggs, but they weren't about to tell the twins that.

'And why do you take that silly-looking dog with you?'

Ana had to be held back. No one called her

precious Fish silly and got away with it. The last time that had happened was in the park. There was a boy there, called Ganpat, who bullied everybody. When he saw Fish he began to tease him.

'Bowow! Bowow! Bowowowow!' he barked in Fish's face. But Fish did not respond. He had started barking, but he still did it only rarely.

'Why doesn't he bark?' Ganpat asked Ana.

'He doesn't like to bark,' Ana said.

Ganpat guffawed rudely. 'Who's ever heard of a dog who doesn't like to bark? Where'd you get him? Silly dog! You should call him Silly. Silly! Silly! Silly!'

The next thing he knew, Ganpat was on the ground, being pounded by Ana. He still had a bald patch where Ana had pulled out a clump of hair in the course of their fight. Everyone called him Ganju Ganpat now. His hair would grow back, but the name would stay with him forever.

'Don't call him silly!' she said to Beena now, while Zain and Sameera held her.

'Ignore them!' said Sameera. 'They're monkeys.'

Zain made chattering sounds.

'Maaaaa!' Meena shouted and ran away inside to complain.

Beena slipped through the gate and followed them, asking questions. 'Has the dragon gone? Why do you go there every day? What's the name of your dog? Is he the adorable orphan pup? Did Adopt-a-pet give him to you? Did your mother allow you keep him, then? Why is he so quiet? Doesn't he bark?'

Finally, Sameera told her to shut up.

Beena started saying, 'I'll tell my ...' but then she decided she'd rather go to the pool with them than go home to tell her mother who would then tell her not to play with Zain and Ana.

They reached the pool and set up their usual watching place. It was more than two months since they had discovered the dragon eggs, and Fish had nearly drowned. The eggs would hatch any day.

Fish was part of Ana's family now.

At first, Dr Nirmala had found it hard to convince Mrs Bopanna. But then Ana said, 'He's just like a fish.'

'Like a fish?'

So Dr Nirmala told her all about how Fish thought he was a fish. Mrs Bopanna laughed so much that she had tears coming out of her eyes and nose. Finally, she took a long breath, and said, 'Some things are inevitable.'

Then she started giggling again, so no one understood what she meant. Dr Nirmala seemed to get it, though, because she winked at Ana and said, 'Now you have fish and Fish!'

As for Fish, he was very happy. At first, Ana was afraid to let him near the fish bowl. But he had got over his urge to jump into water, and was quite content to lie on Ana's bed and gaze into the bowl at Socrates, Plato and Aristotle the Second for hours together. He had the quiet, happy temperament of a fish, and he was no trouble at all. He ate whatever they gave him, though he still preferred fish food.

He lay now, with his head on Ana's lap. She and Sameera were reading as usual. Zain was making a skyscraper out of sticks. He'd given Beena the job of finding sticks, which she was quite happy to do.

It was peaceful and quiet, when suddenly Beena squealed.

'What?' asked Zain. Ana and Sameera were deeply engrossed in their books and paid no attention.

'What's that?' asked Beena, pointing. 'There's something running there!'

They all stood up now. From the turtle's nest to the water's edge there was a blur of movement. When they went closer, they saw the babies. There

seemed to be dozens and dozens of them and they were all scurrying towards the pool as fast as they could.

The children laughed to see them.

'Goodbye, dragon babies!' Zain called out.

'All the best, dragon hatchlings!' called Ana.

'They're not dragons,' Beena said. 'They're turtles.'

'Du-uh!' said Zain and Ana together.

Fish barked.